The Last Book

Written by Lisa and Dallas Lewis

Illustrated by Dallas Lewis

Silly Billy's Mother Whispered, "Silly Billy, Silly Billy. Wake up. It's time to go to the Library."

"But Mom," Silly Billy mumbled half asleep, "It's Saturday. Just this one Saturday can't I just do whatever I want to do?"

"One Hour! One hour at the library, and then you can do whatever you want to do, " his mother replied.

So, Silly Billy dragged himself out of bed, got dressed, and headed for the library.

As Silly Billy neared the library, he saw something very strange. A giant, fiery, fast moving thing was flying through the air. Silly Billy ran as fast as he could to get a better look.

Suddenly, a huge spaceship stopped right over the library. It dropped a very long tube. Then, library books burst through the windows. The long tube sucked them up like a giant vacuum cleaner.

Silly Billy said to himself,"What's going on here?" He ran into the building and up the steps to the rooftop.

On the rooftop, smoke blurred his vision. The ground was shaking from the loud sound of the spaceship's engines.

Ms. Malone the librarian yelled, "Come back! Come back with our books! "

But it was too late. The ship was gone and so was every book in the library.

Ms. Malone called the police, the fire department, and her own mother in New York City. She was very scared. The police told her that the ship had taken everything that could be read in the entire town. She started to cry. Silly Billy couldn't help but smile. With no books in the library he could leave and do whatever he wanted to do, and that is just what he did.

First Silly Billy went to see his friend Big Jim play baseball. When he arrived at the baseball field, the coaches were screaming and yelling at each other.

"Big Jim," Silly Billy asked, "Why aren't you guys playing?"

"Listen," Big Jim said, looking at the coaches.

Big Jim's coach said,"He's out!"

The other coach blasted,"He's safe!"

Big Jim's coach said,"Get out your rule book, you'll see!

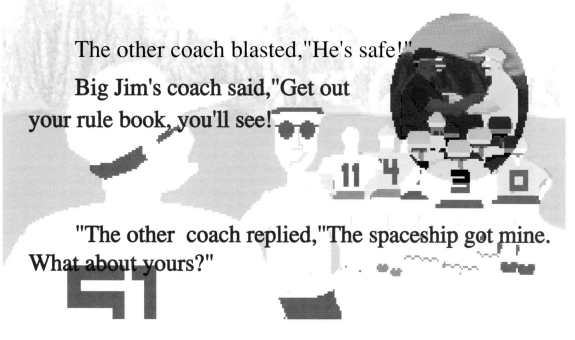

"The other coach replied,"The spaceship got mine. What about yours?"

"It got mine too,"said Big Jim's coach.

" I guess we'll just have to cancel the game until we get the rule books back," one coach said.

Silly Billy said to himself,"No game at this park. I guess I'll just go down and see Captain Rogers at the airport. She always lets me in the control tower to watch the planes fly." And off he went.

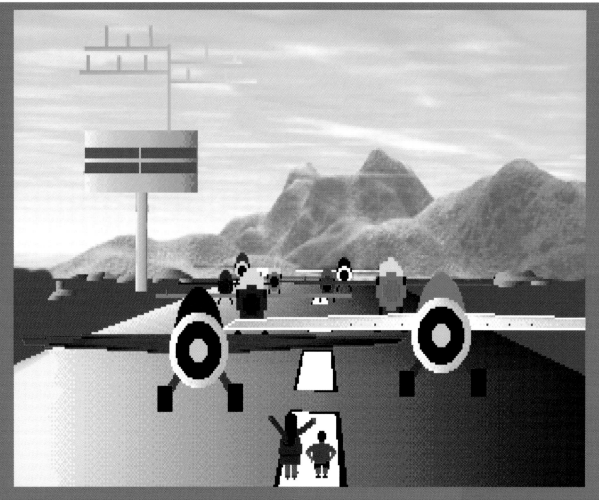

When Silly Billy arrived at the airport, all of the planes were on the ground and Captain Rogers wouldn't let them fly.

Silly Billy asked,"Captain Rogers, Why are you stopping the planes?"

Captain Rogers said, "The Spaceship took everything. We don't have any maps or charts, or landing guides. Without them the pilots aren't able to fly their planes. All flights are canceled until we get them back." She added,"Sorry, Silly Billy. Look! Here's a dollar. Go down to Ethel's Store and have some ice cream on me. OK?" she said softly.

Silly Billy smiled, thanked Captain Rogers, and off he went to Ethel's Store.

When he got there, Ethel's Store was closed. The spaceship had taken all of her price books. Ethel didn't know how much anything cost. She closed the store until she could get her price books back. People waited, and waited outside her store.

Silly Billy couldn't wait anymore. "This is boring. I think I'll go to the Super Mall. They're setting up the rides for the carnival today," he said to himself. So off he went to the Super Mall.

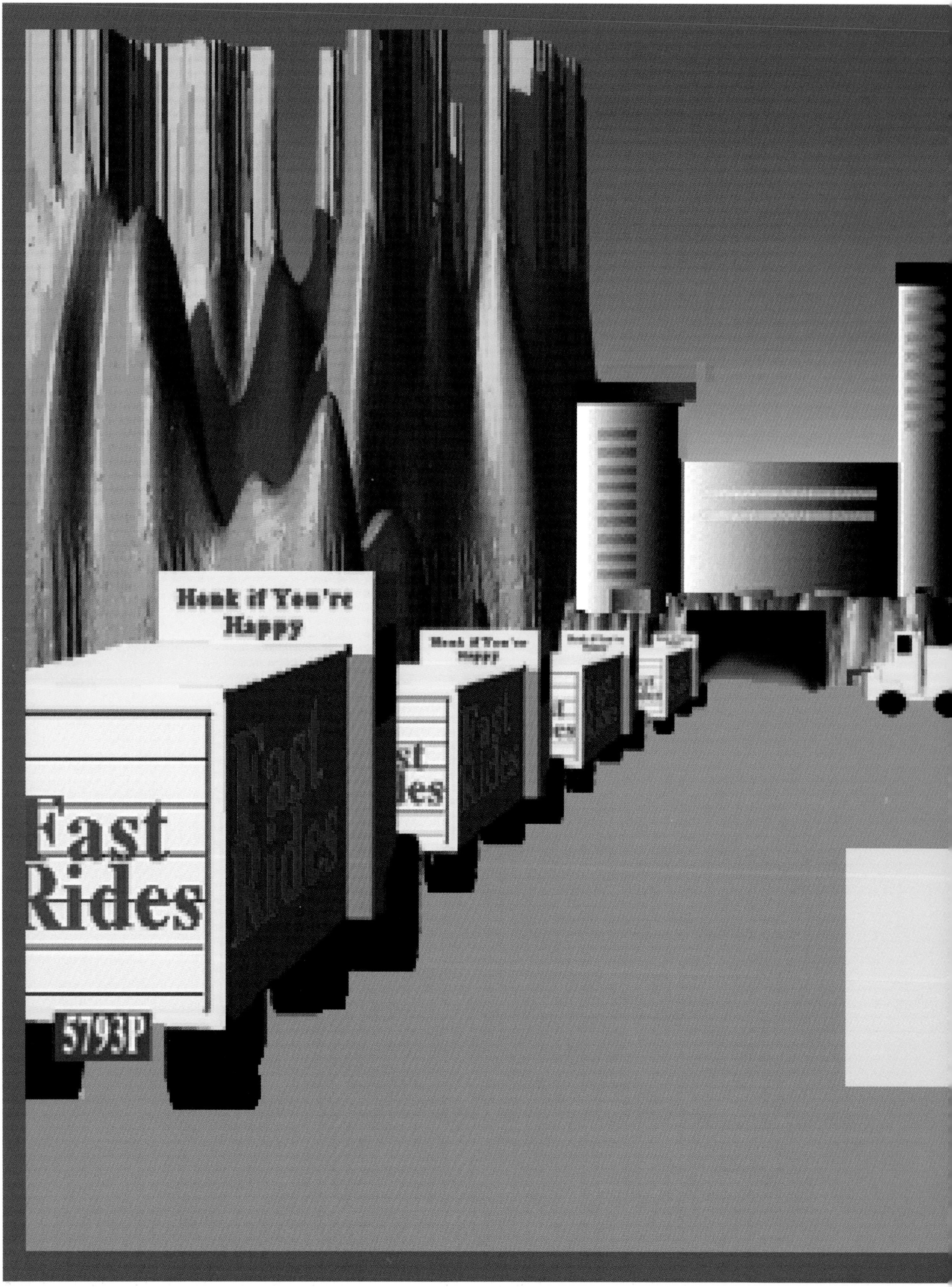

Super Mall

All of the carnival trucks were at the mall, but the people that build the rides didn't have directions to put together the marry-go-round, or the roller coaster or the whippit, whappitt, shake-it, snap-it ride.

Silly Billy moaned, "Give me a break. There must be some-thing fun to do. I'll head over to Juan's house. Juan always has fun."

On the way to Juan's house, Silly Billy saw all of his friends. They looked very happy. Silly Billy asked, "Hey, you guys! What's going on?"

They chanted, "No school Monday! No school Monday! The spaceship took all of the school books."

Silly Billy said, "I knew something good had to come out of this."

All of the kids were happy, except for four, old, high school seniors.

Silly Billy asked,"What's wrong with you guys?"

The first said, "I was going into the Army."

The second added, "I was going to college."

The third replied, "I was going to write music for a big music group."

The last piped in, "And I was going to be a rocket scientist." Then he said, "But with no books, we can't study."

They all said together, "We can't finish school until the books come back!"

Silly Billy shook his head and headed off to Juan's house.

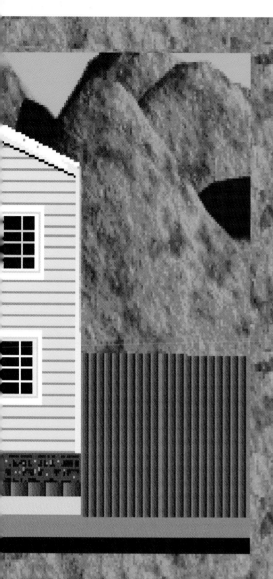

When Silly Billy arrived at Juan's house, Juan was outside crying. He asked, "Juan, why are you crying?"

Juan said, "It's my mother Silly Billy.   She's in the hospital. She's so sick that the doctors can't figure out what's wrong with her.   If they don't figure it out soon, who knows how sick she will get.. The spaceship took all of the doctor books and now they have nothing to read to help them find out what's wrong with her."

Silly Billy was very sad as he left Juan's house. He said, "This book thing is causing a lot of problems. I didn't know it would be like this."

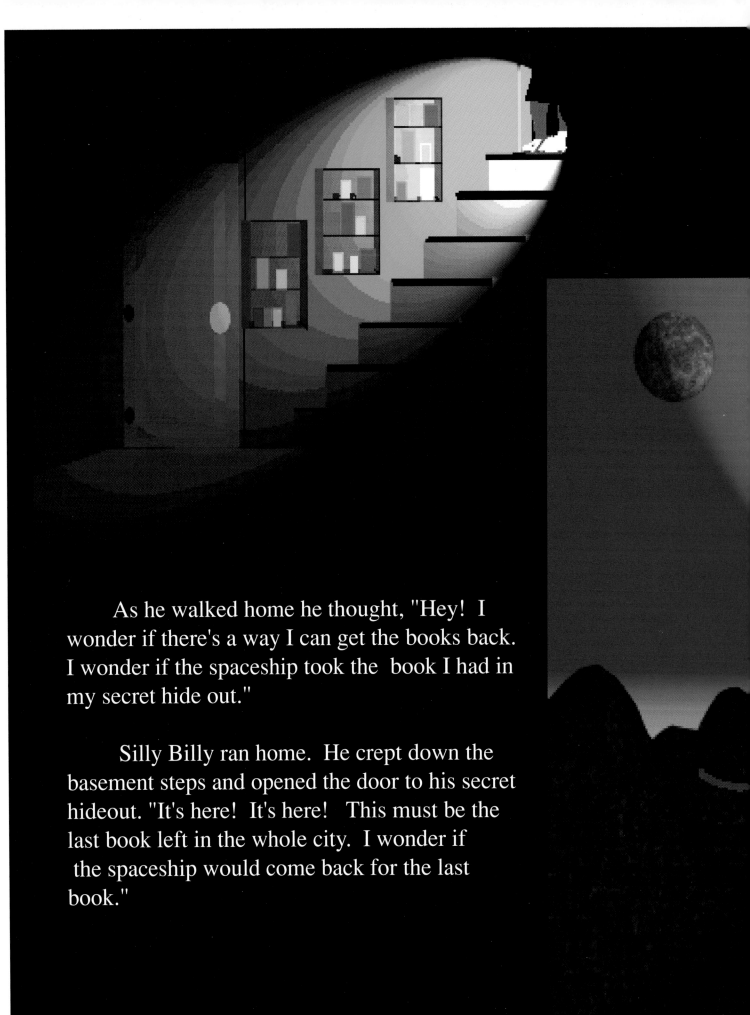

As he walked home he thought, "Hey! I
wonder if there's a way I can get the books back.
I wonder if the spaceship took the book I had in
my secret hide out."

Silly Billy ran home. He crept down the
basement steps and opened the door to his secret
hideout. "It's here! It's here!   This must be the
last book left in the whole city. I wonder if
 the spaceship would come back for the last
book."

Silly Billy took the last book out to the mountain tops. There he waited for hours and hours and hours. Silly Billy stood on the highest peak, holding his flashlight and the last book.

"It's not coming," he sighed. "I guess this was a silly idea. I may as well just go home."

As he started to leave, he could feel the book being pulled up into the air. It almost got away from him, but he held on with all his might.

The next thing he knew, he was flying up through the clouds and the stars, clutching the book tightly. Suddenly, he saw the spaceship and the same long tube that sucked the books from the library. He was forced into the tube, and sucked in deeper and deeper until......

He popped out of the tube. He found himself in a huge room filled with books.

"Hey you!" he heard a strange voice scream.
"What do you think you're doing?" He looked up and
saw a strange girl with purple hair.

"Get out! Get out of here right now!" She added, "If I hit this button Earth Boy, you'll go so far out into space that you'll never get back home."

"Don't! Don't hit the button," Silly Billy pleaded. "Who are you?"

The strange girl said, "I'm Barb-a-barb-a-bab-a-dad. They call me Barb. Who are you?"

Silly Billy replied,"I'm Silly Billy. Ba,ba,ba,,,,Barb? Could you tell me why you took the books?"

She said,   "Ok. I'll tell you why, but then you must leave!"

Barb explained, "On the planet that I'm from, there are only two cities. One city had the Magic Papers, and the other city had none."

Silly Billy asked, "Magic Papers, do you mean these books?"

She said, "Magic Papers! Magic Papers! That's what they are. Say it! Say it! Magic Papers!"

"Ok! Ok! Ma, Ma, Ma, Magic Papers," Silly stuttered.

She said, "The city with the Magic Papers could do anything it wanted to do. Its people would get an idea, look at the Magic Papers and the papers would show them how to make their dreams come true. They had fun, nice houses, and stories to tell. They laughed all of the time."

Then she said, "But the city without the Magic Papers couldn't learn anything. Its people lived in caves and were bored to tears."

Barb added, "One day, my city wanted the Magic Papers too. A big argument started, but I escaped on this spaceship. I knew that somewhere I would find my own Magic Papers."

Silly Billy said, "Come on, you have this great spaceship and you just sit up here and read all day. That doesn't sound like much fun to me."

"Come look," she told him.

"The Magic Papers showed me how to build my very own Super Sweets Machine. With this thing I make chocolate milk shakes, candy bars and nut cakes," Barb said happily. She hit some buttons and out came big, double dip, ice cream cones. The space girl and Silly Billy ate them and talked.

She asked, "Would you like to ride the roller coaster I built using the Magic Papers?"

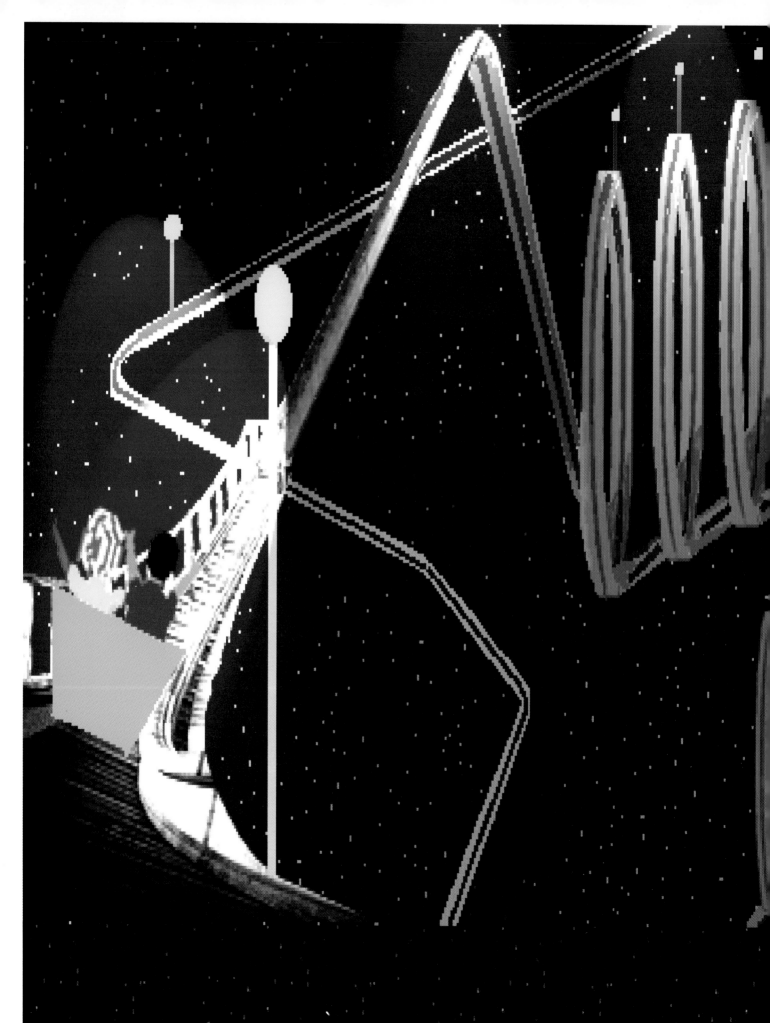

"Sure," he said and off they went.

Down and down and up, then twist and turn. They yelled and laughed.

Silly Billy asked, "And you did all of these things by reading those books? I mean the Magic Papers?"

Barb replied, "With the Magic Papers, I can do anything that I want to do, and it's so much fun."

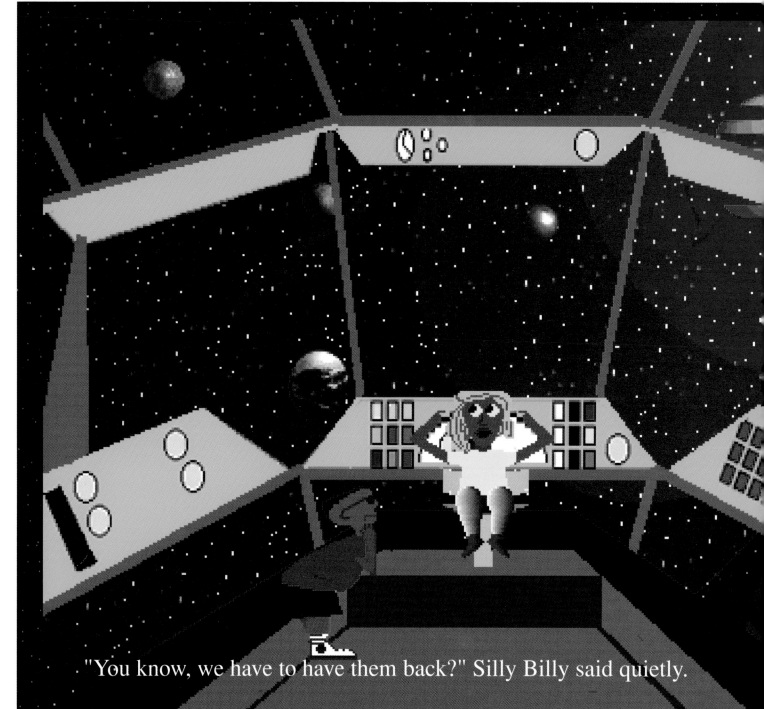

"You know, we have to have them back?" Silly Billy said quietly.

"You want them back?" Barb said with anger, "Are you kidding? Your people don't even like to read. I bet you don't even like to read, do you?"

Silly Billy stammered, "Well uh, uh. That was before I saw how much fun you could have with them."

Barb said, "You see, I don't want to be bored all of the time like the people in my city. With some imagination and the Magic Papers, I become magic, and the magic will take me anywhere I want to go."

Silly Billy stopped and began to think. He asked, "Look! If I could help you and the people from your city use the Magic Papers anytime you wanted to, could we make some kind of a deal?"

"Maybe," she replied.

Silly Billy talked Barb in to flying him back to earth. Then he took her to see Ms. Malone at the library. Ms. Malone was startled to see the space girl with purple hair.

"What can I do for you and your friend, Silly Billy?" She asked.
He said, "Ms. Malone, This is Barb-a-barb-a-bab-a-dad, and she and her space buddies would like to have.........library cards."
And the deal was made. Ms. Malone gave Barb and all of her friends library cards. Barb gave all of the books back. And all of the problems in town were solved..

The coaches at Big Jim's baseball game read their rule books and finished the game.

Captain Rogers at the airport got her maps and charts back and the planes flew again.

Ethel, at Ethel's Store, got her price books back and people could shop again.

The rides were built at the carnival and it was a big success.

Carnival

The high school students finished school and went on the do the things that they had always wanted to do.

Welcome Home
Mom!!!!!!

And finally, the doctors read the books that doctors read and they cured Juan's mother. They fixed her up like brand new.

And now, the very end of the story.

Now every Saturday, Barb-a-barb-a-bab-a-dad and all of her friends, pick up Silly Billy and all of his friends, and they all go to the library and have fun reading the Magic Papers.

Moral

Even Space creatures know it's true. By using the Magic Papers, anyone can do anything. Have fun making yourself Magic. Read, then read more.

The End